**Bedtime Tales
includes:**

Milly the Meerkat

Little Penguin

**Bedtime
on the Farm**

Hiku

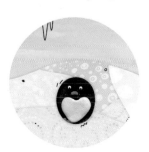

Cub's First Winter

The Silent Owl

Milly the Meerkat

Written by Oakley Graham
Illustrated by Alexia Orkrania

For Noah

There once was a young meerkat called
Milly, who was bored as she sat on an earth
mound taking her turn as lookout.

To amuse herself, Milly took a great, big breath and barked out, "Snake! Snake! A snake is approaching the baby meerkats' burrow!"

All the other meerkats came running out of their own burrows to help Milly drive the snake away.

But when they arrived at the top of the mound, they found no snake. Milly laughed at the sight of their angry faces.

"Don't bark 'snake,' Milly,"
said the other meerkats,
"if there's no snake!"

Later that day, Milly was feeling even more bored and barked out again, "Snake! Snake! A snake is approaching the baby meerkats' burrow!"

To her mischievous delight, Milly watched as the other meerkats rushed to the mound to help her drive the snake away.

But when the other meerkats arrived at the top of the mound, they found no snake. Again, Milly laughed at the sight of their angry faces. "Don't bark 'snake,' Milly," repeated the other meerkats, "if there's no snake!"

Late in the afternoon, Milly saw a REAL snake slithering close to the baby meerkats' burrow.

Alarmed, Milly leaped to her feet and barked out as loudly as she could, "Snake! Snake! A snake is approaching the baby meerkats' burrow!"

But the other meerkats just thought that Milly was trying to fool them again, so they didn't come out to help her.

Outside, as day turned to night, everyone wondered why Milly hadn't returned for dinner. They went to look for Milly and found her crying on top of the lookout mound.

"There really was a snake here! The meerkat babies have scattered! I barked out, 'snake' as loudly as I could," sobbed Milly. "Why didn't you come to help me?"

A wise old meerkat tried to comfort Milly
as they walked back to the village.
"We'll help you look for the lost meerkat babies,"
he said, putting his arm around Milly.

"You have learned an important lesson today, Milly.
Nobody believes a liar...even when they are
telling the truth!"

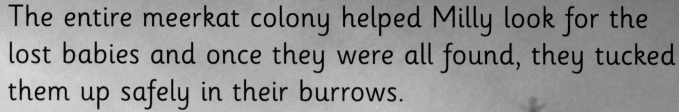

The entire meerkat colony helped Milly look for the lost babies and once they were all found, they tucked them up safely in their burrows.

Milly was very sorry for what she had done and promised that she would never lie to her family and friends again.

Little Penguin

Written by Eilidh Rose

Illustrated by Dubravka Kolanovic

It was an
important day
for Little Penguin.

He was going swimming for the very first time!

Little Penguin was **nervous** about learning to swim...

but he wanted to **Splash** and play with his friends.

So he started to slowly waddle along the icy path toward the big, blue ocean.

Little Penguin was shuffling through the snow, practicing flapping his flippers and **wiggling** his feet, when he saw Little Bird hopping toward him.

"I'm learning to fly!" said Little Bird.

"Are you Scared?"

asked Little Penguin.

"Not really. I'm not very good yet,
but I can almost get off the ground,"
said Little Bird proudly.

Little Penguin continued down the icy path to the ocean.
Suddenly he saw a black shadow on the fluffy white snow.

High above him in the bright blue sky

was Little Bird, twirling

and Swooping through the air.

"I'm finally flying!"

Little Bird squawked happily.

As he was practicing Wiggling his feet,

Little Penguin heard a splash and Little Seal

jumped up on the ice beside him.

"I'm learning to fish!" said Little Seal, happily.

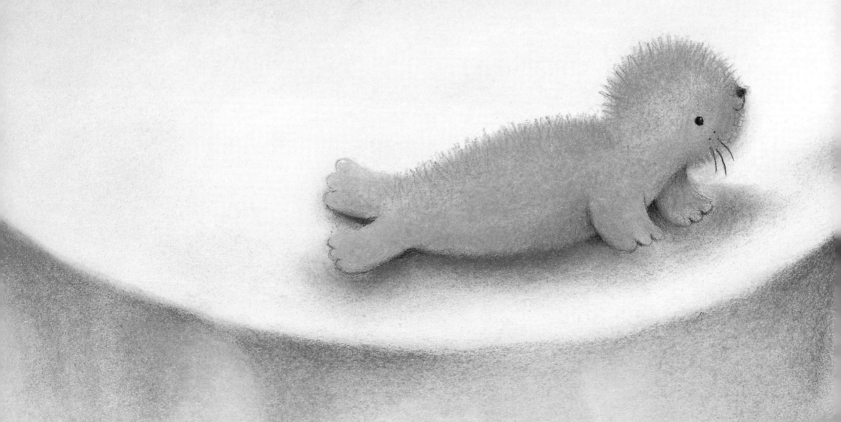

"Are you *nervous?*" asked Little Penguin.

"Not really. I haven't caught anything yet, but it's lots of fun!"

Little Seal saw a school of fish swimming past, so she quickly plunged back into the water.

Waddling on, Little Penguin heard a big

splash

and an excited shout.

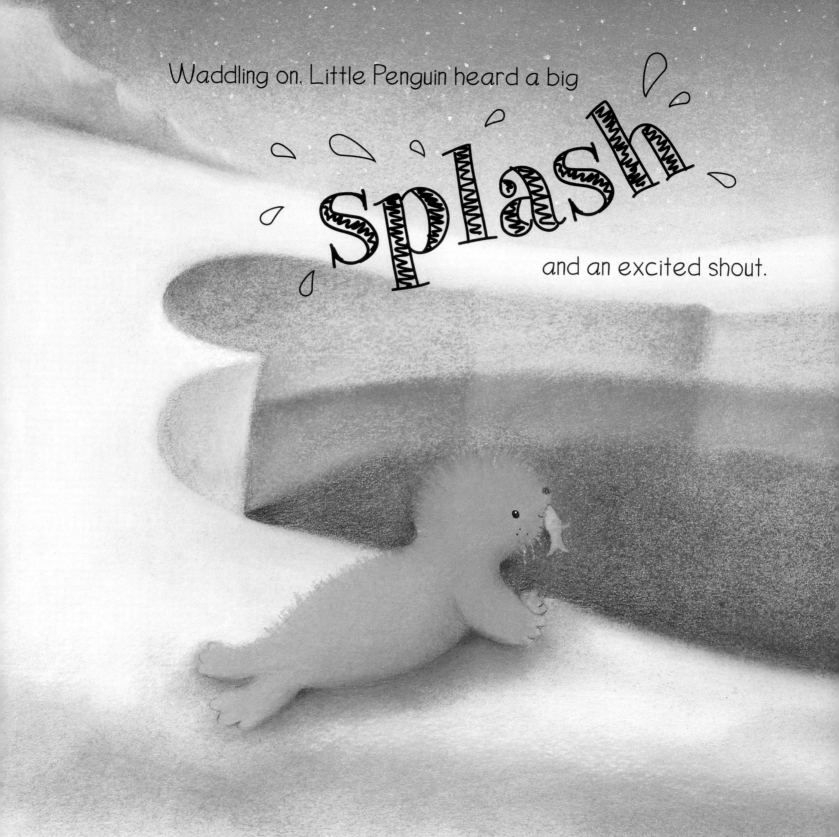

"Look, Little Penguin!"

cried Little Seal. "I caught a fish!"

Little Seal **whizzed** off to show all of her other friends.

Little Penguin felt tired
so he sat down for a rest.

As he was sitting on the ice,
a big wave splashed him.

"Sorry, Little Penguin," said Little Whale.

"I'm learning to jump."

"Are you scared?"
asked Little Penguin.

"Not really. So far I've only done bellyflops,

but I can almost get high enough for big jumps,"

said Little Whale, weaving through the waves.

As Little Penguin got to his feet and shuffled on,

he saw a shape jumping high above him.

It was Little Whale, leaping above the waves!

"Look at this one!" cried Little Whale, somersaulting through the air.

Little Penguin was still worrying about
how to **flaP** his flippers and **wiggle** his feet.

He could see all of his friends splashing and sliding into the water, playing lots of fun games.

Little Penguin **waddled** to the edge
and looked down into the deep, dark water.

It looked **very cold** and he didn't want to go in.
But then he thought about his friends and how
they were not scared to learn new things.

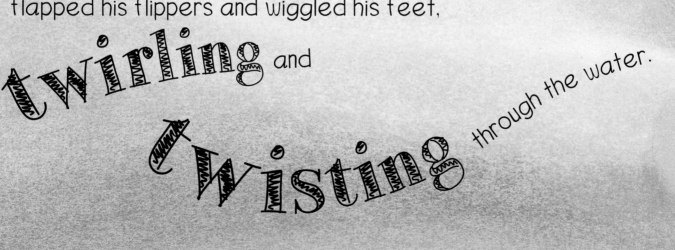

Little Penguin shuffled closer and,

with a deep breath, slid on his tummy

and slipped easily into the water.

Just as he had practiced, Little Penguin

flapped his flippers and wiggled his feet,

twirling and

twisting through the water.

Little Penguin **whizzed** over to his friends to join in with their games.

Even though he had been nervous before,

Little Penguin could not wait to come

back for more fun tomorrow!

Bedtime on the Farm

Written by Corinne Mellor
Illustrated by Karen Sapp

Farmer Jack stands with his dog by the gate,
He looks at the sky—it's getting quite late.
"Time to get everyone back home for bed,
Let's round them up and then get them all fed."

"I need my dog's help," says old Farmer Jack.
"His name is Fred and he helps lead the pack."
High up in the tree, two small kittens mew,
"Jump down," says Jack, "the line starts with you!"

Can you count one dog and two kittens by the farm gate?

They come to a field where Fred stops and pauses.
There eating the grass are three pretty horses.
"Come join us," Jack says. "Please get into line,
This journey back home could take us some time!"

Can you count three pretty horses in the field?

They all follow Jack; the kittens are mewing,
To a field full of flowers where four cows are chewing.
Fred looks at the cows and then starts to bark,
"We've got to go home—it's getting quite dark!"

Can you count four cows in the meadow?

They walk in a line along a small track,
Jack and Fred lead with the cows at the back.
Then up a small hill that's not very steep,
They collect Jack's five fluffy sheep.

Can you count five fluffy sheep on the hillside?

At the top of the hill, where the green grass gets thinner,
Six billy goats are all eating their dinner.
"Let's get you home and give you some hay,"
Says Jack to the goats as he leads the way.

Can you count six billy goats on the hill?

They all tread downhill as the light starts to dim,
To a river where ducks and fish like to swim.
Jack's seven ducks are splashing about,
"Come on, quacking ducks—it's time to get out!"

Can you count seven ducks around the river?

They follow the river along a small path,
Where eight muddy pigs are having a bath.
Farmer Jack frowns before shaking his head,
"I'll clean you all up before going to bed!"

Can you count eight pigs on the muddy bank?

All of the animals come to a stop.
They've reached a hill with nine hens at the top.
"Come on, little hens, not far to go!"
Jack says as he spies the farmyard below.

Can you count nine hens on the hill?

At last! The animals arrive at the yard,
It's been a long walk, and they're very tired.
And although it's near the end of the day,
There are ten little mice still hard at play.

Can you count ten mice in the yard?

It's bedtime on the farm, so why don't you look,
And count all the animals that you met in this book?

Goodbye!

Hiku

Written by Nicole Snitselaar
Illustrated by Coralie Saudo

Hiku, a little penguin,
was feeling grumpy one
morning.

It was one of those days, when the ice was too bright,
the sun was too hot, and his mommy woke him up too early.
"Don't forget that all of our family are visiting today!"
she reminded him.

Oh no! A family visit was the last thing Hiku wanted!
Smiling, greeting, being polite, and listening to,
"You look so cute with your white heart-shaped tummy!" all day.
Or having everyone sing, "Hiku, Hiku, say cheese or you'll freeze!"
Why had he been given such a silly name!
"I want to be alone," grumbled Hiku.

Hiku !

Hiku !

Hiku !

Soon, Hiku saw his family arriving, some by sea, some over the ice field. Hiku slipped past without being noticed and waddled to his hiding place. "At last!" he whispered with relief, snuggling into his special snow hole.

"It's so nice to have some peace and quiet," thought Hiku.
But, very soon he grew bored and lonely.
Sitting in his hiding place, Hiku started to think of some
happy times that he had spent with his family.

That wonderful day at the swimming pool...
sliding, playing, splashing, getting soaked!

Diving deep underwater,
searching for lost treasures.

All the fun and laughter of playing hide-and-go-seek.

Climbing and performing acrobatics at the adventure park.

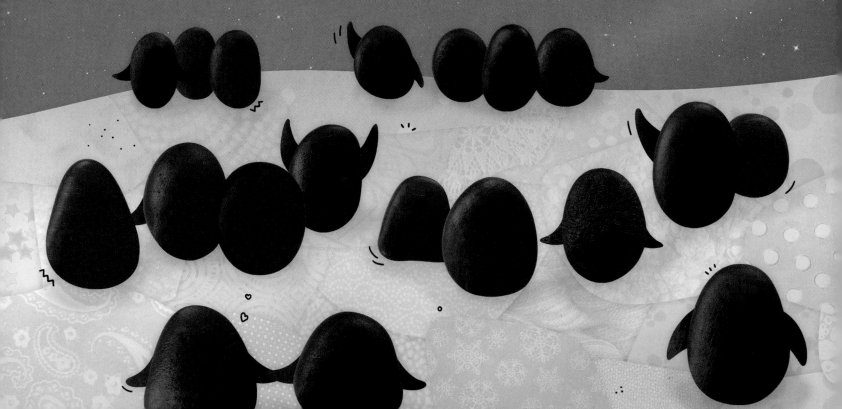

That time, when full of wonder,
Hiku and his family huddled together,
watching the Southern Lights.

And those evenings in front of the blazing fire...

grilling fish and listening to scary stories.

"Oh, what fun my family and I have together," sighed Hiku.
"What am I doing here all by myself?
I hope it's not too late..."
And, without a second thought, Hiku waddled back to join his family.

Hiku arrived just in time for the family photo!

"Ready? 1, 2, 3...Hiku!" said the photographer.
"Hiku, Hiku, say cheese or you'll freeze!" laughed everyone.
"A name that makes your family smile isn't that bad!" thought Hiku,
and he joined in with the family fun and games.

Say goodbye, Hiku.

Cub's First Winter

by Rebecca Elliot

"For Mum and Dad who have always taken
such good care of their own cubs. x"

It was the first day of winter
and Cub could not sleep. "OK," said Mom.
"One more forest walk before bed. Come on…"

"Why are all the trees undressed?" asked Cub.

"So that we can have fun in the leaves!" answered Mom.

And the snow clouds gathered in the sky.

"Why are my friends asleep all the time?" asked Cub. "Ssshhh! So that we can laugh at their snoring!" giggled Mom.

And the first snowflake fell to the ground.

"Why are the birds
going on vacation?" asked Cub.
"So they can tell us all about their
journey when they come back!" said Mom.

And the snow began to gently fall.

"Why is it so windy?" asked Cub.
"So that we can be blown about together
in the tall grass!" laughed Mom.

And the snow drifted down.

"Why can I see my own breath?" asked Cub.
"So that we can puff like steam engines!" puffed Mom.

And the snow began to settle on the ground.

"Why is the river solid?" asked Cub.
"So that we can slide and dance on it!" exclaimed Mom.

And the snow fell more quickly.

"Why does the sun disappear so early?" asked Cub.
"So that we can look up at the stars for longer," explained Mom.

And the snow got deeper and deeper.

"Why is everything white?" asked Cub.

"Oh no!" gasped Mom.
"Quick, follow me before we lose our way home!"

And back they went through the white forest,
over the white river, up and down the white rocks,
and around and around the white trees until,
at last, they found their way home!

"Why is it so c-c-cold?"
asked Cub.

"So that we can
snuggle up tight,"
whispered Mom,
with a smile.

"Why am I so tired?"
yawned Cub.
"Because it is sleepy time,"
murmured Mom.
"Sleep tight little cub."

The Silent Owl

Written by Clemency Pearce
Illustrated by Sam McPhillips

For Rob and Silkie—Sam
For Gemma, the noisiest bird I know—CP

In the great old hollow oak,
Lived an owl who never spoke.

Fox asked, "Why do you never speak?"
But Owl refused to move his beak.

Badger huffed, "How very rude!"
But Owl would not, could not, be moved!

A swooping bat whooped, "Say hello!"

But Owl was silent far below.

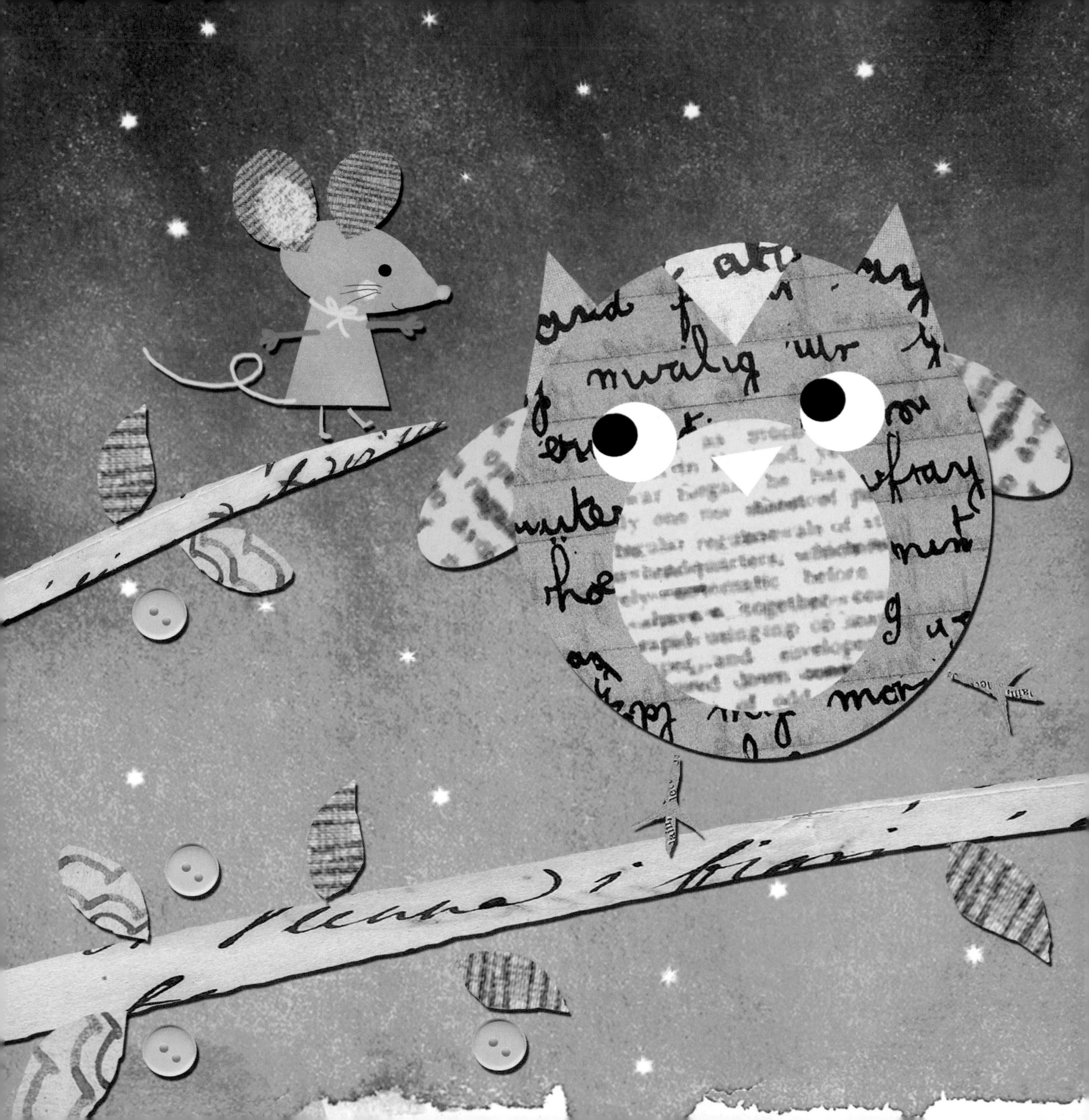

A pair of mice squeaked in his ear,
"Is it that you cannot hear?"
But Owl just rolled his giant eyes,
And stared up at the starry skies.

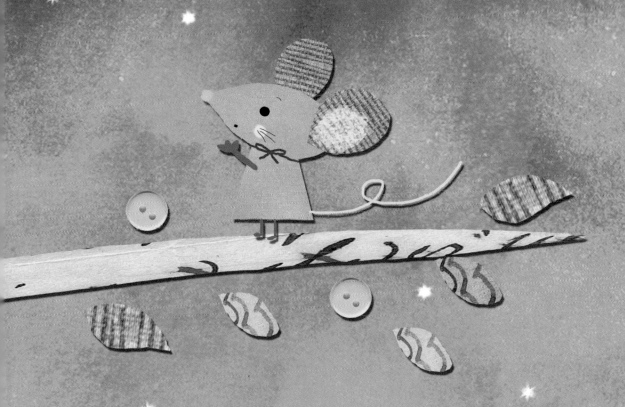

Squirrel scolded, "Are you nuts?"
But Owl ignored his toothy tuts.

Rat cried, "Owl! This isn't right!"
But Owl just gazed into the night.

Stag said, "Owl! We need a sign,
To let us know that you are fine."

So all the creatures gathered around,
To see if Owl would make a sound.

They stared at Owl; he stared right back.
Who would be the first to crack?

Stag declared, "He must be mute,
Or he doesn't give a hoot!"

At this, the owl produced a trumpet,
A big bass drum and stick to thump it.

Although Owl wouldn't hoot,
he played the bongos,

piano,

guitar,

and flute!

The animals cheered, "What a clever bird!"
And Owl just winked without a word.